ARCHIE'S LOOSE TOOTH

by Henrietta Stickland

RAGGED BEARS PUBLISHING

One hot day in the outback
Mitzi came across
Archie standing by the
waterhole, perfectly still,
**with a book
balanced on
his head**.

"Archie, why have you got a book on your head?" she asked.

"To stop my head from wobbling," explained Archie.

Archie demonstrated how his head was wobbling by holding his tooth with his finger and gently wobbling his head **backwards and forwards**.

"You're right!"
exclaimed Mitzi.
**"You need help,
fast! This is
an emergency."**
So Mitzi took Archie off
to find the Koala Brothers
to see if they could help.

Frank and Buster were also puzzled as to why Archie had a book on his head.

"Archie needs help, **his head's wobbling**, so I brought him here," said Mitzi.

"Well you've come to the right place," said Buster, comfortingly.

"Mmmm, perhaps it's your tooth that's wobbly . . . not your head," said Frank.

"Why don't you try holding your head still and wobbling your tooth?" he suggested.

Archie gave his tooth a careful wiggle.

"Well look at that!" exclaimed Mitzi.

wobble wobble wobble

"See Archie, it must be a baby tooth. That's what they do, they get loose and then they fall out!" explained Frank.

"It's nothing to worry about Archie, once your tooth falls out, **a lovely new tooth** will grow back in its place!"

wobble

wobble

wobble

wobble

Archie **was** pleased his head wasn't wobbling.

But no matter how hard he tried he couldn't stop worrying about his loose tooth. Everyone noticed how unhappy he looked. **"What's up Archie?"** asked Buster.

"It's this tooth . . . I'm worried about it falling out and it leaving a gap . . ." sighed Archie.

"**It'll fall out** when it's ready, Archie," explained Frank.

"And it won't leave a gap for long. We just need to take your mind off it for now," he added.

wobble

wobble

wobble

wobble

"What do you like doing best?"

Buster asked Archie, helpfully.

Archie thought about it and replied, "I love jogging, and tennis and all kinds of sporty things really."

"Right!" said Frank and Buster and they set about taking Archie's mind off his tooth.

First of all they
sent Archie off
jogging,

but his
loose tooth
wobbled
too much . . .

Then Archie played **tennis**,

but it was too hard for him to play while he was holding his tooth . . .

Archie felt even **more miserable**.

"Is there anything else you like doing?" the Koala Brothers asked him.

"Well, I like having my photo taken,"
he replied, and with that Mitzi rushed off to get her camera.

Archie, Frank, Buster and Ned stood in a group and waited for Mitzi to take the picture.

"Ned, duck down a bit! **I want to get a good picture of Archie's tooth**," she said.

With that, Archie's smile faded and he started fiddling with his tooth and worrying again.

Now Archie couldn't do three things he really loved.
He couldn't go jogging, he couldn't play tennis, and he couldn't
have his photograph taken. All because of his loose tooth.

wobble
wobble
wobble

The friends all tried to think of something else to take Archie's mind off his tooth. **"I've got an idea!"** said Frank. "Let's take Archie up in the plane."

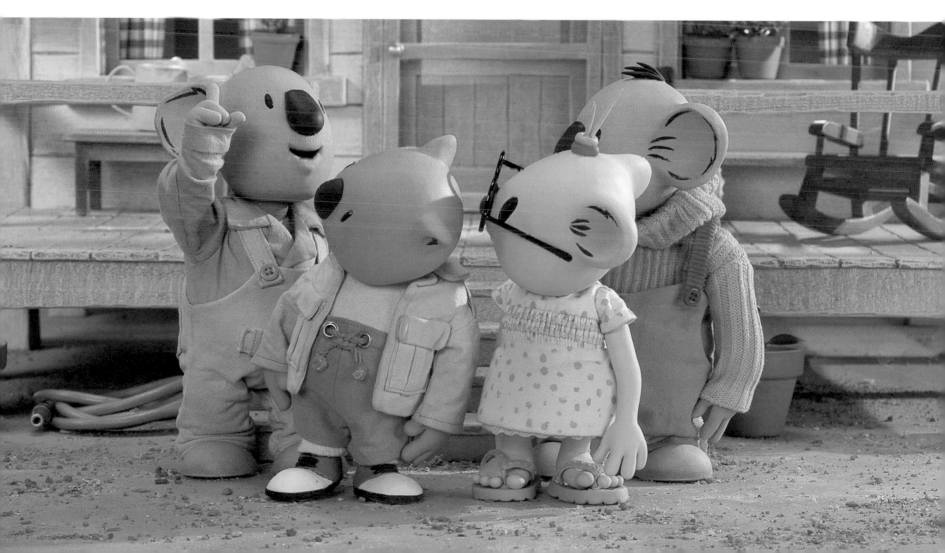

After all, how could you worry about a loose tooth when you are flying up in the clouds, thought Frank?

But the plane made Archie's tooth wobble as well and as soon as Frank saw Archie wasn't enjoying it, he just had to land.

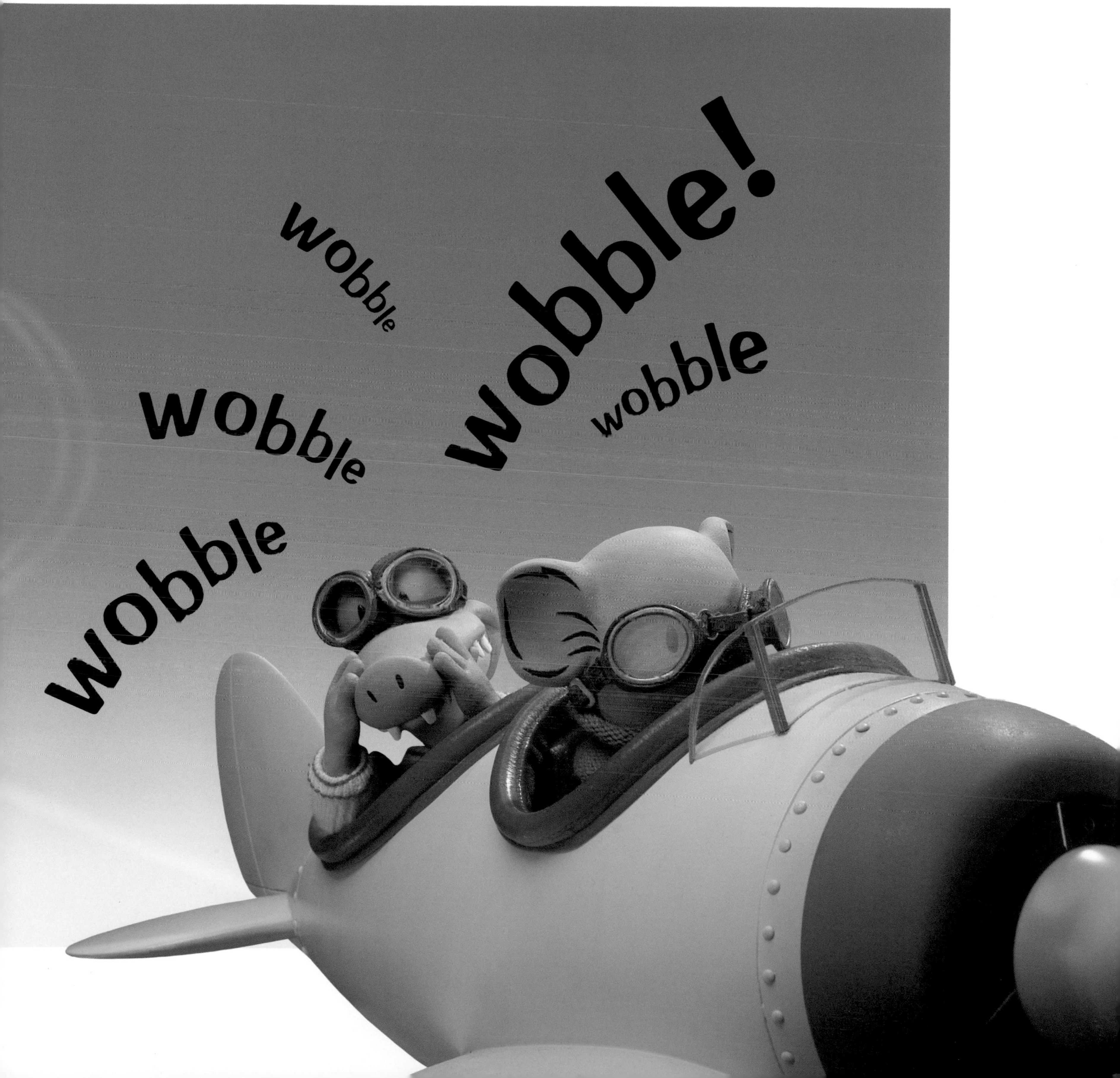
wobble
wobble
wobble
wobble!
wobble

The friends just didn't know **how to distract Archie**.
They were sure they had thought of everything, when suddenly
Buster read the title of the book that had been on Archie's head.
"Party games!" he said.

"Oooh I love party games. My favourite is apple bobbing! I'm really good at it," said Archie, excitedly, flashing a toothy smile.

So they set a barrel up in the yard, filled it with water and apples and everyone had a go. No one was very successful, so Archie helpfully bobbed an apple for all of his friends.

He was having such a good time, he'd forgotten all
about his wobbly tooth.

"**What's this?**"
asked Mitzi as she
pulled something out
of her apple.

"Archie, your tooth!"
cried Frank and Buster.

"**My tooth!
My loose
tooth has
fallen out!**"
said Archie.

Archie realised that losing a tooth wasn't that bad after all. And when his tooth did grow back it was

bigger

and brighter than ever before!

Copyright © 2007 Spellbound Entertainment Ltd. and Famous Flying Films Ltd.
First published in 2007 by Ragged Bears Publishing Ltd.,
Milborne Wick, Sherborne, Dorset DT9 4PW
www.raggedbears.co.uk

Distributed by Ragged Bears Distribution, a division of Publishers Group UK
8 the Arena, Mollison Avenue, Enfield, Middlesex EN3 7NL. Tel: 020 8804 0400

Based on the original television script by Dave Ingham

A CIP record of this book is available from the British Library

ISBN 978 1 85714 379 9

Printed in China

www.koalabrothers.com